William Trumbull, Frank V. Du Mond

The Legend of the White Canoe

William Trumbull, Frank V. Du Mond

The Legend of the White Canoe

ISBN/EAN: 9783337391898

Printed in Europe, USA, Canada, Australia, Japan

Cover: Foto ©Andreas Hilbeck / pixelio.de

More available books at **www.hansebooks.com**

THE LEGEND

OF

THE WHITE CANOE

BY

WILLIAM TRUMBULL

WITH PHOTOGRAVURES FROM DESIGNS BY

F. V. Du MOND

G. P. PUTNAM'S SONS
NEW YORK   LONDON
27 WEST TWENTY-THIRD STREET   24 BEDFORD STREET, STRAND
The Knickerbocker Press
1894

Electrotyped, Printed, and Bound by
The Knickerbocker Press, New York
G. P. Putnam's Sons

DEDICATED

TO

A. L. T. T.

Long before the solitudes of western New York were disturbed by the advent of the white man, it was the custom of the Indian tribes to assemble occasionally at Niagara, and offer sacrifice to the Spirit of the Falls.

This sacrifice consisted of a white birch-bark canoe, which was sent over the terrible cliff, filled with ripe fruits and blooming flowers, and bearing the fairest girl in the tribe who had just attained the age of womanhood.

CONTENTS

v

ILLUSTRATIONS

Illustrations

I.

PROEM.

MID the rush of mighty waters, in the thundering
    cataract's roar,
Where Niagara's streaming rapids down in headlong
    torrent pour;
Where the serried waves like chargers madly leaping
    to the fray,
Fling aloft their snowy crests and toss their manes of
    flying spray,
Rearing, plunging, onward urging—Nature's glorious
    cavalry !
Where th' eternal sweep of waters like the unending
    surge of time,
Pulsing, throbs in rhythmic measure to a wondrous
    strain sublime :
Dwells, so ancient legends say, the mighty Spirit of
    the Falls,
Who from out the tumult, hoarsely, for unbounded
    homage calls.

* * * As often as they listened, on the voices of the flood,
Deep were borne the Spirit's mutterings, calling fierce
for human blood.

Here the children of the forest, spellbound by that
    deafening roar,

Stopped to gaze with listening wonder, in the simpler
    days of yore ;

Awe-struck, gazed in silent worship, well beseeming
    Nature's child,

As in chase they roamed the plain, or tracked in war
    the pathless wild :

And as often as they listened, on the voices of the
    flood

Deep were borne the Spirit's mutterings, calling fierce
    for human blood ;

Ay, and sacrifice more cruel in that cry they under-
    stood :

Gift of Nature's choicest treasure, peerless budding
    womanhood !

II.

WENONAH.

FAIREST of the laughing daughters by blue Sene-
    ca's rippling tide,

Was the Indian maid, Wenonah, sturdy Kwasind's joy
    and pride:

Eyes of laughter, like the sunshine dancing in her
    native lake,

O'er whose depths, anon, fleet shadows chasing cast
    their trailing wake;

Lips of tempting ruddy hue like mountain berries
    gleaming fair;

Raven locks, whose glossy lustre shone like dark-stem-
    med maidenhair;

Whilst rich mantling color tinged an olive cheek, whose
    crimson flush

Vied with flaming woodland leaves when touched with
    Autumn's scarlet blush.

She, hailed queen by all the maidens, led with merriest quip and song.

And the music of her laughter, when amid the joyous
  throng,
She, hailed Queen by all the maidens, led with merriest
  quip and song,
Fell in sweetest rippling cadence, sounding thro' the
  leafy way
Like the purl of hidden brooklet murmuring soft in
  distant play;
As in freest fancy roving, far removed from cares or
  strife,
With fresh eager zest exulting in youth's bounding
  sense of life,
Bright she moved, a winsome picture, framed by
  Nature's matchless art
In all scenes of joy and beauty royally to bear her
  part.

Yet to scenes of mirth not solely was her sunny
presence lent ;

Truer was her simple nature, to a nobler purpose bent :

Only child of widow'd father, hers the sacred heritage,

With the charm of winning girlhood, to make bright
his lonely age.

What tho' ardently, nay fiercely, for her smiles the
young braves strove

In all feats of savage daring—none as yet might claim
her love ;

She, with roguish, artless spirit, laughing in her gay
caprice,

Found in loving, filial duty surer joys of heart-whole
peace.

9

Just as when some sturdy giant of the forest, bending
low,

Bows before the axe and toppling falls with mighty
crashing blow,

Clinging tendrils, newly springing round the shattered
trunk are seen

Swift to hide its prostrate ruin 'neath a veil of living
green,

Guarding, shielding, closely nestling to their riven
parent stock,

Like mute sentient creatures fearful of rude gaze or
heedless mock :

So the maid her lonely father tended with fond, jealous
pride,

Steadfast, faithful to her trust, where none might woo
her from his side.

Grave attention holds the band.

III.

THE COUNCIL.

GATHERED is the warriors' council. Thro' the
  shadows of the night,
Darkly gleams each dusky figure in the camp-fire's
  fitful light.
Slowly round the silent circle moves the red-pipe's
  gleaming bowl,
Thro' whose clouds each wreath'd sage, peering the
  dark future to unroll,
Draws a drowsy, sweet contentment, for the moment,
  o'er his soul.
Now, the brooding hush is broken; grave attention
  holds the band,
For the Med'cine-man is speaking of the want through-
  out the land;
Slow, in subtle craft, contrasting with the wealth of
  happier days
Present dearth of fish and venison, withering blight
  upon their maize.

Well he speaks! His halting manner but betrays the
    deeper art
Of his cunning soul vindictive; which full oft had
    conned this part,
Since that day when in dim forest glade Wenonah
    spurned his quest,
And with flaming scorn repelled the love his suppliant
    words confessed.
Little recked the fearless maiden in that lonely, fateful
    hour,
Dark appeal, mute, threatening gesture, hints of baleful
    fetich power;
For while untaught reason wavered, blindly groping
    toward the light,
Woman's faultless intuition read his lying heart aright!

"Senecas! Twice the rolling Autumn, with deep-laden
malice fraught,

Years of blight and wasting sickness to your golden
maize hath brought.

Yet again the dread plague threatens! Speak, deluded,
hapless race,

Will ye, reckless, longer trust th' uncertain product
of the chase?

Hunted, driven, the startled red deer, fleeing, vanish
from your sight!

Hark, the cry of fenland wild-geese, parting on their
southward flight!

E'en your lake trout, lurking wary, yield but scanty
livelihood—

Will ye see your children starving? Answer, Senecas!
Is it good?

Came the Spirit of the Waters, wreathed in billowy clouds of spray.

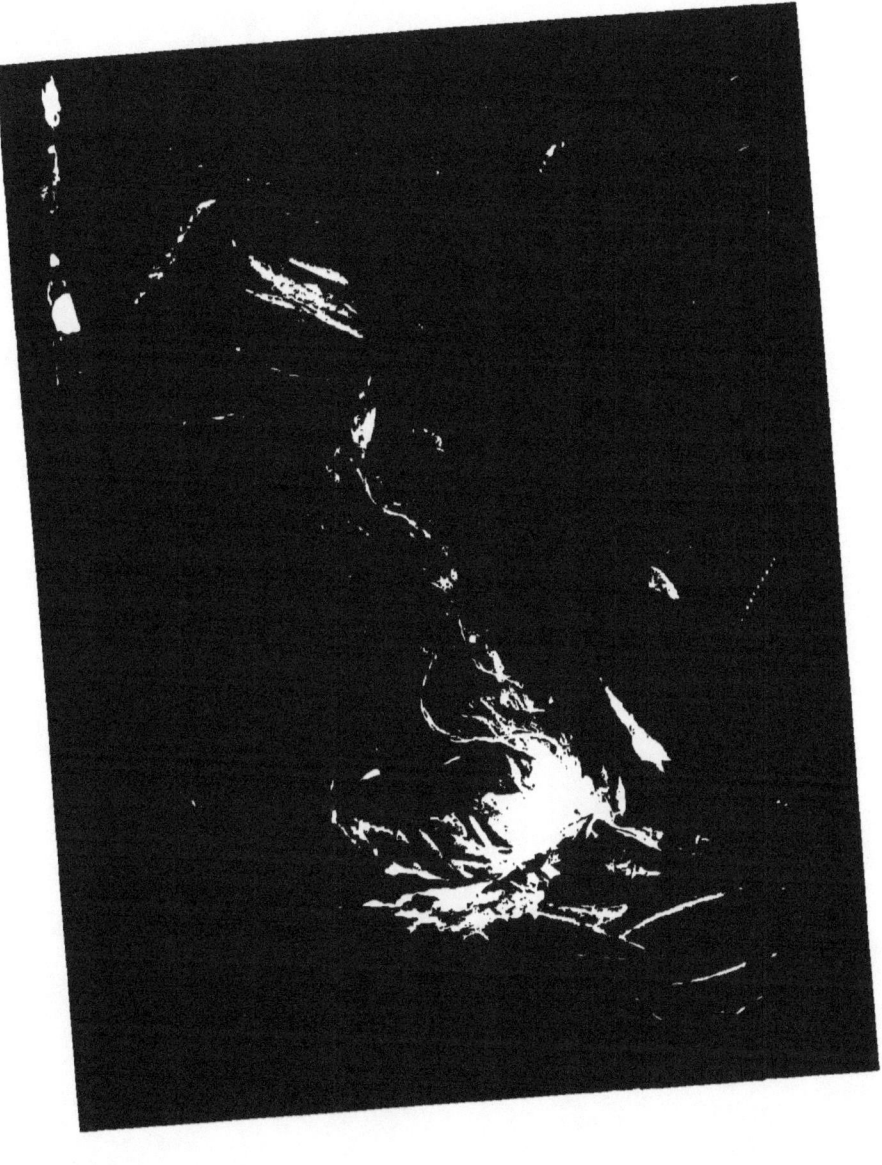

"Listen! To your dreaming Meda, while in troubled
   sleep he lay,
Came the Spirit of the Waters, wreathed in billowy
   clouds of spray :—
'Wherefore do My children shun Me? Where the
   grateful offering rare
Of the maid and first-fruits choicest, which they once
   were wont to bear?
Has *prosperity* thus turned them from the faith of
   simpler days?
Let them heed, lest FAMINE seal My warning blight
   upon their maize!'
So He spake, with muttered thunderings, leaving me
   as one for dead.
Need I counsel? Heed the warning! Yet delay not!
   —I have said."

Ceased the speaker, 'mid a silence, chill, foreboding as the grave,

Save where some sage, nodding grayhead growl of half-conviction gave,

As at grim want's threatening horror, fear, by ghastly memories fed,

Woke to flame the smouldering embers of a cruel faith nigh dead;

Or perchance, some young brave, chafing sore in hot, rebellious mood,

With the first warm flush of manhood 'gainst a bygone creed of blood,

Carried past his wiser fellows, borne by love's impetuous stream,

Muttered curse both deep and savage on the Meda's boding dream!

But all eyes were fixed on Kwasind, Strong Man,
warrior proved and true,

Whose brave heart, where others faltered, never fear
nor weakness knew ;

Hero of a thousand conflicts, scarred in visage, proud
of mien,

Foremost ever in rude battle, chase, or stirring council-
scene :

And their eyes were fixed upon him with a deep,
expectant gaze,

Watching for some answering signal which their
sinking hearts might raise ;

Hope and terror strangely blended in that wistful,
furtive stare,

Not unmixed with curious pity for a father's mute
despair !

Long they sat, in silence waiting.   Neither word, nor
   sign, nor glance
From the Sachem came in answer to their wondering
   look askance.
—Ah! the nameless, unseen terror of that shadowy
   Spirit-land,
With its spectral shapes and phantoms,—who its power
   can understand?
Now, in sudden wrath he starts at thought of pity from
   the rest,
Crushes down the welling tumult surging thro' his
   anguished breast,
Cloaks 'neath stoic, outward calm the grief he struggles
   to control—
Lest perchance he may betray the finer feelings of his
   soul!

There he sits, all wrapped in silence, strangely mute, impassive grown,

Drawn each stern and rigid feature like carved lines of chiselled stone ;

Iron will and haughty spirit bravely answering to repress

Quivering lip and trembling eyelid,—signals of his deep distress.

See ! he meets their searching glance with head erect and flashing mien ;

Slowly gazes round the assembly with unflinching air serene :

Victor in th' unnatural conflict ; love and nature, both defied ;

Slave to coward superstition ; thrall of idle savage pride !

* *

IV.

KWASIND.

NOR when, once the conclave over, striding back in anger wild

To the hut, where all unconscious of her fate, his darling child

Rose to greet his late home-coming,—did his flood of grief long-pent,

In a burst of manlier feeling find, e'en then, its fitting vent :

But in tones of measured calmness, self-repressed, and sternly brief,

He made known his tidings bitter to her gaze of wondering grief ;

Nay, to that grim ordeal, harshly, bade her nerve her trembling frame,

For the welfare of her people, for the honor of his name !

Yet, in lonely midnight vigil, when beneath the unwonted
  strain,
Baffled nature rose rebellious, throbbing fierce in secret
  pain,
Vowed he threat of direst vengeance, breathing forth
  an ominous hiss
'Gainst the doting, idle dreamer :—"Curse him, he
  shall die for this !"
Or as tenderer feelings, rushing with tumultuous ebb
  and roll,
Stirred to ruth the deep recesses of his inmost troubled
  soul,
Pity for her youth and beauty, doomed thus soon to
  fade and die,
Found expression mute yet touching, in a long-drawn
  secret sigh.

Or he dwelt on her obedience, on her silent fortitude,

Bowing to his will submissive, 'neath a blow so harsh and rude :

And it called to mind her mother, gentle slave of days long fled,

Slain, alas ! in hostile foray ere *her* noon of life had sped.

How might she have met this trial ?—What her thought of him, who must

In the pride of false endurance, thus betray a father's trust ?

'Till proud spirit, bowed in anguish, brooding thro' the silent night,

Staggered 'neath the strong temptation of a swift, inglorious flight.

Then, a sterner mood returning, pride resumed its
   wonted sway ;
Bade him heed the tribe's opinion ; pictured what his
   braves might say :
While he strove, with specious reasoning, which he well
   knew for a lie,
To assuage the qualms of conscience—outraged nature's
   stifled cry !
Her obedience ?—but th' expression of a flattered vanity
At the tribute of the council's silent unanimity !
Or if here, too, justice triumphed, muttered with con-
   temptuous thought :
" After all, she 's but a woman !"—and in this a respite
   sought.

Slow was borne into the village by the young braves of the band.

So the days dragged slowly onward, days of strife and
  varying mood,

As he watched her steadfast bearing from his gloomy
  solitude :

And one morn, the treacherous Meda, slain by hostile,
  unknown hand,

Slow was borne into the village by the young braves of
  the band.

None mistrusted sullen Kwasind, when the funeral
  throng drew nigh,

Or, at least, none cared to question with that scowling
  warrior by.

But th' event was soon forgotten 'mid the press of other
  calls,

And the stir of preparation for their long march to the
  Falls.

V.

THE SACRIFICE.

COME, at length, the fatal evening—for such purpose, all too soon !
—On a scene of matchless glory slow uprose the harvest
moon :
Crested wave and shimmering islet, bathed in flood of
golden light,
Caught and threw its tremulous radiance far adown the
wind-kissed night ;
Soft the mellow moonbeams glinting thro' the leaves
on isle and shore,
Spread beneath, their quivering fretwork, interlaced with
shadows o'er ;
Now, the full orb's splendor shining, woke to brilliant
glistening play
Myriad hues of emerald richness, showers of sparkling
diamond spray.

On the cliffs beyond the cataract, ranged like sentinels
    on high,
Giant trees stood darkly shadowed, spectre-like against
    the sky ;
Far beneath, the seething river, wrapped in deepest
    midnight gloom,
Flowed with cruel, swirling torrent thro' the gorge—a
    fitting tomb !
While, like ponderous portals clanging 'twixt these
    scenes of death and life,
Boomed the Falls, their bellowing echoes telling of
    a ceaseless strife ;
Riven, torn in wildest fury, lashed to foam and clouds
    of spray,
Like some clamorous monster raging for its long-
    expected prey.

From the shore, in jarring discord with the spirit of the
hour,

Shouts of revelry invaded its sublime, mysterious
power :

Man, the slave of passions rude, in superstition's yoke
enthralled,

Marred the face divine of Nature, by her grandeur
unappalled.

—There they danced in wild carousal, thro' that
glorious moonlit night,

Love and friendship all forgotten, in their orgies' fierce
delight ;

Thinking thus, poor simple children, best the dread
wrath to assuage

Of that Spirit dark, whose roaring told of boundless,
sullen rage.

Hark! a distant shout. Swift following, comes a
　　momentary hush.
Then, their ill-timed revels quitting, to the river's bank
　　they rush :
Up the stream all eyes are straining, toward yon faintest
　　speck of white,
Where the frail birch onward dancing, flashes in the
　　moon's pale light :
Large, now larger, grows the object ; till at length the
　　kneeling form
Of a maid is seen, her tresses blowing wildly in the
　　storm ;
Clasped her hands, her lips half-parted, staring down
　　the angry stream
As if spellbound by the horror of some hideous night-
　　mare dream !

At that sight, their spell is broken. Cheer rever-
berates on cheer,
Till the answering banks re-echo like a scoffing, mocking
jeer.
Louder still their cries redouble, as the skiff with
frightful lunge
Leaps in where the steadier current gathers for its final
plunge.
Passed the head of low-crowned Iris! Luna gleams!—
But what is this?
Why this stillness, broken only by the thunder of th'
abyss?
Why this sudden pause from shouting, and that swift-
averted gaze
To yon point where, circling, eddying past the shore,
the current plays?

Shooting straight to meet his fellow, lo! a second skiff
they spied.

Leaping from the mainland outward, darting, bounding
    o'er the tide,

Shooting straight to meet its fellow,—lo ! a *second*
    skiff they spied.

Mark the dripping blade flash brightly, scattering drops
    of silver light,

As the shallop plunges, lurches, forward urged by
    desperate might !

See ! it nears ; they strike !—Defiant, stands a swaying,
    stalwart form ;

Poises high the useless paddle ; hurls it at the ravening
    storm !

While an arm protecting, shielding, round the startled
    maid is flung :—

"'T is her father ! Kwasind ! Kwasind !" bursts in frenzy
    from the throng.

* * * *In his tender, yearning eyes,*
Clear she reads the pregnant meaning of that love-
wrought sacrifice.

Ay; 't was Kwasind! Love, triumphant over every
 fear and doubt,
Love had won the final victory, putting stubborn pride
 to rout.
By that one brief glance at meeting, in his tender
 yearning eyes,
Clear she reads the pregnant meaning of that love-
 wrought sacrifice :—
Not forgotten, not forsaken, in that lonely, bitter hour !
Then, tho' certain death await her, answering to his
 love's strong power
Leaps the light of new-born gladness in her eyes !—
 With quickened breath,
Clasped as one, they pass the portal to the shadowy
 realm of death.

51

VI.

EPILOGUE.

AND in after years, at nightfall—still the Indian
    legends say—
When each swift revolving Autumn brings again that
    fatal day,
From Niagara's brow, a shallop thro' the dusk is seen
    to glide,
Stemming with unwavering course the mighty flood's
    on-rushing tide ;
Till, a jutting headland reached, it swerves, and nears
    the northern strand,
Where a slight form, dimly shadowed, on the bank is
    said to stand :
There, its strange freight once embarked, it veers, and
    downward thro' the night
Bears the spectral, kneeling figure of a maiden robed
    in white.

Where in strong love clasped together, father, daughter
fading sink.

And as often as the phantom nears the head of
    Luna's shores,
From the bank, another shallop leaps to meet its gliding
    course ;
Swift by frantic stroke impelled, it intercepts it near the
    brink,
Where in strong love clasped together, father, daughter,
    fading sink :
And as surely as they vanish, louder roars the Spirit
    gray ;
Higher yet, like incense rising, waft the rolling clouds
    of spray ;
Whilst the moon, her pale face veiling high in Autumn's
    cloud-flecked skies,
Mourns the unending expiation of that cruel sacrifice.

www.ingramcontent.com/pod-product-compliance
Lightning Source LLC
Chambersburg PA
CBHW022013050726
47499CB00007BA/2572